NICHOLAS ALLAN

JESUS' CHRISTMAS PARTY

Mini Treasures

RED FOX

For Richard McBrien

5 7 9 10 8 6 4

First published in the United Kingdom 1991
by Hutchinson Children's Books
First published in Mini Treasures edition 1996
by Red Fox
Random House Children's Books, 61-63 Uxbridge Road, London W5 5SA

Random House Australia (Pty) Limited
20 Alfred Street, Milsons Point, Sydney,
New South Wales 2061, Australia

Random House New Zealand Limited
18 Poland Road, Glenfield,
Auckland 10, New Zealand

Random House South Africa (Pty) Limited
PO Box 2263, Rosebank 2121, South Africa

Random House UK Limited Reg. No. 954009

A CIP catalogue record for this book
is available from the British Library

ISBN 009 9725 916

Printed in Singapore

There was nothing
the innkeeper liked
more than a good
night's sleep.

But that night there was
a knock at the door.

'No room,' said the innkeeper.
'But we're tired and have travelled
through night and day.'
'There's only the stable round the back.
Here's two blankets. Sign the register.'
So they signed it: 'Mary and Joseph.'

Then he shut the door,
climbed the stairs,
got into bed,
and went to sleep.

But then, later, there was
another knock at the door.

'Excuse me. I wonder if
you could lend us
another, smaller blanket?'

'There. One smaller blanket,'
said the innkeeper.

Then he shut the door,
climbed the stairs,
got into bed,
and went to sleep.

But then a bright light
woke him up.

'That's ***all*** I need,' said the innkeeper.

Then he shut the door,
climbed the stairs,
drew the curtains,
got into bed,
and went to sleep.

But then there was ***another***
knock at the door.

'We are three shepherds.'
'Well, what's the matter? Lost your sheep?'
'We've come to see Mary and Joseph.'
'ROUND THE BACK,'
said the innkeeper.

Then he shut the door,
climbed the stairs,
got into bed,
and went to sleep.

But then there was yet
another knock at the door.

'We are three kings. We've come —'

'ROUND THE BACK!'

He slammed the door,
climbed the stairs,
got into bed,
and went to sleep.

But ***then*** a chorus of
singing woke him up.

Hallelujah!
Hallelujah!
'RIGHT – THAT DOES IT!'

So he got out of bed, stomped down the stairs,

threw open the door, went round the back,

stormed into the stable, and was just about
to speak when —

'Ssshh!' whispered everybody,

'you'll wake the baby!'

'Baby?' said the innkeeper.

'Yes, a baby has this night been born.'

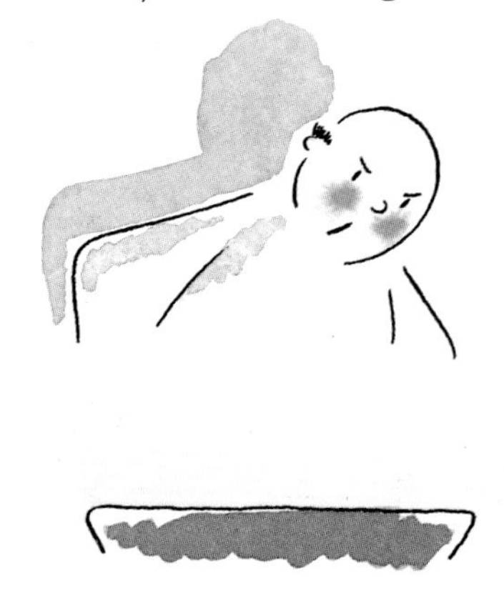

'Oh?' said the innkeeper, looking crossly into the manger.

And just at that moment, suddenly, amazingly, his anger seemed to fly away. 'Oh,' said the innkeeper, 'isn't he ***lovely!***'

In fact, he thought he was so special .

so that they could come an

. he woke up ***all*** the guests at the inn,

have a look at the baby too.

So no one got much sleep that night!

THE END